Dear Parent:

Your child's love of reading starts here!

Every child learns to read in a different way and at his or her own speed. Some go back and forth between reading levels and read favorite books again and again. Others read through each level in order. You can help your young reader improve and become more confident by encouraging his or her own interests and abilities. From books your child reads with you to the first books he or she reads alone, there are I Can Read Books for every stage of reading:

SHARED READING
Basic language, word repetition, and whimsical illustrations, ideal for sharing with your emergent reader

BEGINNING READING
Short sentences, familiar words, and simple concepts for children eager to read on their own

READING WITH HELP
Engaging stories, longer sentences, and language play for developing readers

READING ALONE
Complex plots, challenging vocabulary, and high-interest topics for the independent reader

I Can Read Books have introduced children to the joy of reading since 1957. Featuring award-winning authors and illustrators and a fabulous cast of beloved characters, I Can Read Books set the standard for beginning readers.

A lifetime of discovery begins with the magical words **"I Can Read!"**

Visit www.icanread.com for information
on enriching your child's reading experience.

The Addams Family: A Frightful Welcome
Printed in the United States of America. No part of this book may be used or reproduced in any manner whatsoever without written permission except in the case of brief quotations embodied in critical articles and reviews. For information address HarperCollins Children's Books, a division of HarperCollins Publishers, 195 Broadway, New York, NY 10007.

www.harpercollinschildrens.com
ISBN 978-0-06-294677-5

19 20 21 22 23 LSCC 10 9 8 7 6 5 4 3 2 1 ❖ First Edition

I Can Read!

READING 3 ALONE

A Frightful Welcome

Adapted by Alexandra West
Pictures by Lissy Marlin

HARPER

An Imprint of HarperCollinsPublishers

This is the Addams Family.

They do things a little differently

from other people.

Everyone seems to think that

they are terribly strange.

People seem to be afraid of them!

As you might think,

they don't get many visitors.

Not only does the Addams Family act strange,
but they also have strange names.

This is Gomez and Morticia.

Their children are Wednesday
and Pugsley.

Uncle Fester is Gomez's brother.

Grandma is Gomez's mom.

Lurch is the butler.

Sometimes the Addams Family does act

like other people.

For example, they have a pet.

His name is Kitty.

But Kitty is a lion!

No one wants to come over

with a pet lion lying around!

Morticia and Gomez are madly in love.

Their favorite thing to do together is dance.

These lovebirds are surprisingly

good at dancing.

No one would ever guess

that Gomez has two left feet!

He keeps the two left feet in his closet.

Pugsley loves anything
that is extremely speedy.
He builds his own toys.
He can create things
like powerful rockets.

Sometimes his inventions
aren't very safe.

Wednesday is very smart.

She figured out how to bring

frogs back to life.

She brought a lot of frogs back to life.

Can you imagine

a house full of zombie frogs?

Then we have Lurch.

When he answers the door,

he doesn't make

a good first impression.

His massive height and greenish skin

make people run away.

Some people's manners are

just plain monstrous!

Uncle Fester is strange too.

He comes to visit the

Addams Family from time to time.

Wednesday and Pugsley like him.

He makes for good target practice.

One day, something strange happens.
First, the Addams Family sees
little pieces of paper in the sky.

Then the fog around the house lifts.

Suddenly they see a town!

"We must go down and

introduce ourselves!" Gomez says.

When the family arrives in the town,
they are stunned.
It isn't what they expected at all.
"It's so different!" Wednesday says.

"Who would want to live here?"
Morticia asks, looking at the colorful buildings.
The family has never seen so much
pastel in their lives!

Kitty runs off to play.

When Pugsley sees a dog bowl,

he begins to drink from it!

A man walking by sees Pugsley.

The man stops to stare.

"Come along, Pugsley," Morticia says.

"This man may want some too."

Gomez decides to explore.

He visits a coffee shop.

"Good day, all!" Gomez says.

Gomez orders coffee.

But not regular coffee.

He orders the coffee grounds!

They are black and gunky.

The grounds drip all over his face!

Gomez joins the family.

That's when they see a choir.

Children are singing happy songs.

"Everybody come together," they sing,

"and sing our song!"

All of this happiness and cheer

scares the Addams family!

"They are greeting us!" Gomez says.

"It must be a traditional song."

Uncle Fester wants to sing too.

He pulls out two bats.

Uncle Fester and his bats

begin to sing.

It scares the children!

26

Just then, the Addams Family
meets Margaux Needler.
"Morning!" she says.
"You must be the new neighbors."

Margaux's job is to make the
neighborhood beautiful.
To her, beautiful means
everything looks the same.

Margaux is very pushy.

She even invites herself

over to the family's mansion!

"When should I stop by?" she asks.

"Well . . . actually," Morticia responds.

Gomez clears his throat.

That reminds Morticia that she needs
to give Margaux a chance.

"Stop by any time," Morticia says.

Margaux smiles. "See you soon!"

The Addams Family climb into their car.

It has been a very long day.

They are happy to be heading home.

They are also happy to be together.